The L♥ve~ME BiRd

For the Lovelorn – feathered or not.
JD

To the Shut-Eyes everywhere –
one day, love will touch you too.
SF

Scholastic Children's Books
Commonwealth House, 1-19 New Oxford Street
London WC1A 1NU, UK
a division of Scholastic Ltd
London ~ New York ~ Toronto ~ Sydney ~ Auckland
Mexico City ~ New Delhi ~ Hong Kong

First published in hardback in the UK by Scholastic Ltd, 2003
First published in paperback in the UK by Scholastic Ltd, 2003
This paperback edition first published in the UK by Scholastic Ltd, 2004

Text copyright © Joyce Dunbar, 2003
Illustrations copyright © Sophie Fatus, 2003

ISBN: 0 439 98276 6

Printed in Singapore

2 4 6 8 10 9 7 5 3 1

The rights of Joyce Dunbar and Sophie Fatus to be identified as the author
and illustrator respectively of this work have been asserted by them
in accordance with the Copyright, Designs and Patents Act, 1988.

The L♥Ve~ME BiRd

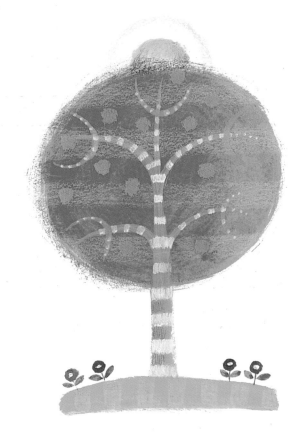

Joyce Dunbar   Sophie Fatus

All was silent in the wood.

Suddenly, out of the green,
"Love-me! Love-me! Love-me!" called the Love-Me bird.
There was no answer to her call.
"Love-me! Love-me!" the Love-Me bird trilled again.
Still, there wasn't an answer.

"Love-me! Love-me!" the Love-Me bird kept on calling,
until she woke up Shut-Eye, the owl.

"Some of us are trying to get some
shut-eye," grumbled Shut-Eye.
"But it's springtime! Wingtime!
Flingtime!" said the Love-Me bird.
"Sing-a-ding-a-lingtime!"
And up she started again.

"Love-me! Love-me! Love-me!"
But though the Love-Me bird sang all day,
and all of the next day too,
there were no answers to her call.

"There must be some-birdy out there,"
she said sadly to Shut-Eye.
"Perhaps you should try another way,"
suggested Shut-Eye.
"Which way?" asked the Love-Me bird.
"Romance. Glad rags. Frippery
and finery," said Shut-Eye.
"That's an idea," said the Love-Me bird.

So the Love-Me bird put on her glad rags.
She plucked and prinked and preened until her wings
were shaped like hearts. She brushed and dressed her crest.
She decked herself with flowers.

"Love-me! Love-me! Love-me!" she warbled, all of a flutter.
Only the leaves fluttered back.
She warbled until she could warble no more.

"It didn't work," she said to Shut-Eye.
"Perhaps you overdid it," said Shut-Eye.
"What now?" asked the Love-Me bird.
"Act helpless," said Shut-Eye,
"then a mate might come to your rescue."

So the Love-Me bird acted helpless.
With crumpled crest and drooping feathers,
she flopped around looking sorry.
"Love-me. Please love-me. Please," she twittered.
There came no twittering replies.

"It didn't work," she said to Shut-Eye.
"No," sighed a very tired Shut-Eye.
"Why don't you play it cool? Play hard to get."

"How do I do that?" asked the Love-Me bird.
"Stick your beak in the air and fly away,"
said Shut-Eye. "Far, far away."

So the Love-Me bird played it cool.
She stuck her beak in the air and flew far away.
But not far enough for Shut-Eye.

"It didn't work," she said, flying straight back.
"No-birdy knew I was hard to get."

"Perhaps you should build a nest,"
said Shut-Eye. "Another Love-Me bird might like it."
"A love-me-nest," said the Love-Me bird.
"A love-each-other-nest," corrected Shut-Eye.

So the Love-Me bird built a nest.
She wove and spun and tweaked and threaded
until she had a fabulous nest in the sky.
She lined it with moss and feathers.
"Love-me! Love-me! Love-me!"
she crooned from her nest.

All kinds of birds flew by.
But none of them looked at her nest.
She crooned all day and all night until
she could croon no more.

"My nest wasn't good enough,"
she said to Shut-Eye. "I'll never be loved."

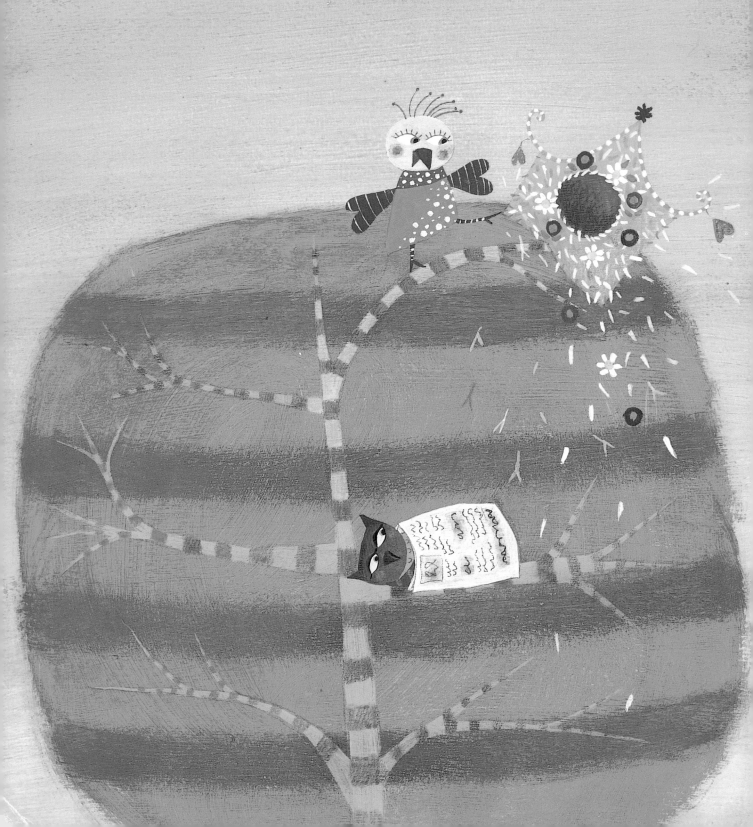

"There's one last thing you can try," said Shut-Eye.
"What's that?" sniffed the Love-Me bird.
"Sing a different tune," said Shut-Eye.
"What tune?"

"How about,
Love-yoo-ooo! Love-yoo-ooo!"
Shut-Eye tu-whitted and tu-whooed.
"But I'm a Love-*Me* bird, not a Love-*You* bird,"
said the Love-Me bird.
"Perhaps you can be both at once,"
winked Shut-Eye. "Try it and see."

Next day, all was silent in the wood until,
"Love-you! Love-you! Love-you!"
called the Love-Me bird from her tree.

Suddenly, out of the blue . . .

"Love-you! Love-you! Love-you!"
came an answering Love-Me bird call.

There was a swoop,

and a flutter of wings . . .

. . . and Shut-Eye got some shut-eye!